A Letter to Anne Frank

A Novella

Aryan D. Ahire

ISBN 978-93-5667-640-4
© Aryan D. Ahire 2023

Published in India 2023 by Pencil

A brand of
One Point Six Technologies Pvt. Ltd.
Unit no. 26, Ground Floor, Building A1,
Wadala Truck Terminal Road,
Near Post Office, Antop Hill, Mumbai - 400037
E connect@thepencilapp.com
W www.thepencilapp.com

Author biography

Aryan Ahire is a curious and ambitious teenager with a deep passion for exploring new things. He is an accomplished writer, "A Letter to Anne Frank" is his first fictional epistolary novella. In October 2021, he published his first non-fiction book titled "The Curb on Infinity," which has been well received by readers, professors, scientists, and critics alike. Aryan's love for technical research subjects is evident in his impressive academic record. He has already published a review research paper in a reputed international journal, demonstrating his exceptional analytical skills and attention to detail.

Currently, Aryan is channelling his writing skills towards topics related to women, democracy, and crime, using his platform to raise awareness and advocate for change. His interests are now turning towards philosophy and literature, where he hopes to continue making a meaningful impact through his writing. Aryan's passion for writing and research is matched only by his dedication to sharing his ideas with the world. If you are looking for thought-provoking and insightful content, Aryan's work is worth checking out.

<u>**Other works by Aryan**</u>

Book: - The Curb on Infinity (https://www.amazon.in/Curb-Infinity-Ethics-Universe-ebook/dp/B09J1QC1ZP)
Research Paper:- Radioactivity (https://journals.resaim.com/ijramt/article/view/2331)
Article 1: - Yes, I was Raped (https://reflections.live/articles/10136/yes-i-was-raped-an-article-by-aryan-ahire-8531-lef5raq5.html)
Article 2: - Yes, I was Bullied (https://aryanahire.blogspot.com/)
Article 3: - Government surveillance(https://www.booksie.com/691426-government-surveillance-and-its-ethical-implications-for-democracy-and-privacy)
Article 4:- Are you a victim of Social constructivism (https://www.booksie.com/691716-are-you-victim-of-social-constructivism)

<u>**Find out more about him at: -**</u>

Twitter: - https://twitter.com/AryanAhire2004
Instagram:- https://www.instagram.com/aryan.ahire1947/
LinkedIn:- https://www.linkedin.com/in/aryan-ahire-0516a4221/
Amazon:- https://www.amazon.in/Aryan-Ahire/e/B09JSJV8BM%3Fref=dbs_a_mng_rwt_scns_share
FB:- https://www.facebook.com/profile.php?id=100090091158848
Blogger:-

CONTENTS

Introduction

<u>This short story is dedicated to Anne Frank.</u>

"Dear Anne, your diary has moved millions, and your legacy has inspired future generations. You have proved the power of the human soul to continue even in the darkest of situations with your strong spirit and constant hope.

This narrative is dedicated to you, Anne Frank, as a memorial to your amazing life and a reminder not to forget history's lessons. May your memory motivate us to fight for a world controlled by liberty, justice, and compassion."

Namaste friends, I thank you for buying my second book. I shouldn't refer to it as a book; it is only a tiny tribute to Anne Frank, my favourite author. I've read her diary almost four times because I adore her writing. I simply turn the pages of her diary whenever I'm depressed. I'll provide a brief biography of Anne Frank for those who are unfamiliar.

World War 2 was a terrible time, and young Anne Frank resided in Amsterdam at that time. To escape being discovered by the Nazis, she and her family went into hiding in a hidden home that she refers to as the "Annex" in her diary. Over the two years that she was hiding, Anne started adding personal entries to the diary that her father had given her on her birthday. In her diary, Anne wrote about her concerns, aspirations, and worries. Her diary has grown into a testament to the human spirit and a sobering reminder of the horrors of war.

I've always been impressed by Anne Frank's story and her capacity for hope and beauty in the face of such hardship. When going through the boxes in my storage room, I accidentally came across a small item: a torn notebook that I had forgotten about. I was astonished to see comments and scribbles about Anne's diary and Anne Frank's life inside when I opened it. Throughout my time at school, I penned these notes and scribbles.

When I read Anne's diary in school, I vividly recall being moved by the strength of her writing. I had never forgotten her narrative, and when I reread my scribbles and notes, I felt a strong connection to her once more.

I understood as I went through the pages that my notes and scribbles were more than just a compilation of facts and observations. They served as a record of my emotional journey as I immersed myself in Anne's narrative. I'd written many imaginary stories in my notebook. "A letter to Anne Frank" was one of the stories. I always wondered how Anne could write such beautifully. My difficulties to comprehend the magnitude of what Anne and her family had gone through was always with me. I felt a renewed feeling of purpose as I went over my thoughts.

At that point, I realized I had to pen this novella. I wanted to look into how Anne's narrative had affected my own life and pay tribute to her memory in some tiny manner. I wanted to create a character like Daisy, who might find hope and solace in Anne's words and share their experience with others.

When I began to write, I discovered that the words came readily to me. Daisy's narrative and her letters to Anne took on a life of their own, and I felt a sense of excitement and exhilaration that I hadn't felt in a long time. It was both a challenge and a pleasure to write this novella, and I am glad for the opportunity to share it with you.

In "A Letter to Anne Frank," I was curious to write about how Anne's narrative has affected characters, notably a young girl named Daisy. Daisy's wartime experiences have left her traumatized and unable to make sense of the world around her. She finds a kindred spirit and a source of optimism in her letters to Anne.

I wish to reassure readers that all revenues from the sale of this novella will be donated directly to war victims. It is my goal that "A Letter to Anne Frank" may encourage readers to consider the power of hope and the human spirit's perseverance in the face of inconceivable circumstances.

With Every Great Wish,

Aryan D. Ahire

:)

Legal Notes

Copyright © [2023] [Aryan D. Ahire]. All rights reserved.
Disclaimer:
The contents of this novella are fictional and any resemblance to actual persons, living or dead, or actual events is purely coincidental. The author has made every effort to ensure the accuracy of the information within this book was correct at the time of publication. The author does not assume and hereby disclaims any liability to any party for any loss, damage, or disruption caused by errors or omissions, whether such errors or omissions result from negligence, accident, or any other cause. The author also does not endorse any products or services mentioned in this novella. Any opinions expressed within are solely those of the author and do not necessarily represent the views of any organizations or individuals mentioned herein.

If you are interested in creating a short film or podcast version of this novella, please contact the author at: -
ahirearyan28@gmail.com

Chapter 1. Family

Dear Anne,

My dad's birthday was today, which is usually a happy occasion for me. I adored my father more than anything in the world; he is my idol. In the morning, I sprang out of bed and ran downstairs to the kitchen to assist my mother in making breakfast. My dad's favourite breakfast was scrambled eggs and toast, which we cooked.

We all exclaimed "Happy birthday!" and sang him a song as my dad entered the kitchen. He seemed shocked and delighted as he grinned widely. As a family, we spoke and laughed while eating breakfast at the kitchen table.

We unwrapped gifts following breakfast. I had been holding onto my pocket money for weeks to purchase my dad a unique present: a photo album with images of the two of us throughout the years. He praised it and gave me a huge bear hug. The remainder of the day was spent getting ready for a small family gathering that evening. My mother prepared a substantial supper, and we garland and balloon the living room. My dad was giddy with joy, and I was pleased to have contributed to making his day memorable.

We all sat down to eat when our family showed up. A chocolate cake was presented by my aunt, and we sang happy birthday once again. I delivered my free verse poetry for my hero after cutting the cake by pulling a page from

my pocket.
Dad, you are my dear lad,
I know you are the sweetest of my heart
I love you from the bottom of my heart,
I know you will not leave me alone like a solitary bird.
For you, I am an angel sent from heaven.
May god bless you and me for the rest of our life.
Everyone applauded after hearing the poem. Dad gave me a forehead kiss. Mum was delighted to see us both. We all convened for dinner after that mother served us all. My mother always ensured that no one should go hungry after leaving this house. I enjoy her food because of her wonderful touch! We spoke and played games well into the night after we had done eating. That evening, when I went to sleep, I was pleased and joyful. I was appreciative of my family and our shared affection. Even though life may be challenging at times, I am confident that we will always have each other to rely on.

My parents had arranged a surprise camping trip for us the next day, a Saturday. My mother and I had spent the morning filling the car with our belongings and our luggage. We were both eager to escape the bustle of the city and spend the weekend in nature. Rolling hills and flower-filled fields were seen as we made our way towards the countryside. I opened the window and took a deep breath, feeling the cold breeze brush my cheeks. As we travelled across the countryside, my mother played some of our favourite songs, and we all sang along.

As we neared our destination, my father pointed out various locations and related tales from his youth. He recounted the camping trip he took with his family and the misadventures they experienced. His tales heightened my anticipation for our camping excursion.

My dad immediately put up our tent at the campsite as my mother and I unpacked the cooler and got to work on lunch. We shared a picnic supper while sitting in the shade of a nearby tree, taking in the sounds of the surrounding forest and each other's companionship.

We decided to go on a trek to explore the region after lunch. We crossed gurgling streams and strolled through verdant woodlands. My dad told us stories and shared his knowledge of the natural world as he pointed out various flora and creatures. We went back to our campground as the day wore on and built a fire. Around the fire, while laughing and joking with one another, we cooked marshmallows and shared stories. Being surrounded by the love of my family and the splendour of nature made me feel pleased.

I experienced a sense of calm as we prepared to spend the night in our tent. I was soothed to sleep by the sounds of crickets and the rustling of leaves, and I was aware that I would recall this camping trip for a long time. I was thankful for my family and the affection we shared at that time.

The following morning, I awoke in our tent while it was still early. We both had a sly glimmer in our eyes, and my mother was already awake. We were both eager to execute the prank we had planned on my dad. My mother and I approached my father, who was still sound asleep in his tent. We carefully positioned the fake spiders and snakes we had brought along around his tent to keep him asleep. We went back to our tent and waited for my dad to wake up after setting up the prank. We could hear him rising and rummaging around in his tent, and we attempted to suppress our laughs as we waited for the prank to take effect.

After that, we heard a loud shout coming from my father's tent, followed by a string of expletives. My mother and I couldn't hold our laughter as we were so amused by his response. We ran over to his tent while laughing and attempting to be sorry. After a while, my dad started to chuckle as well, acknowledging that he had been duped. We had a terrific time making fun of each other all morning long.

I experienced a sensation of bittersweetness as we prepared to leave the campground and packed up our belongings. While I was aware that our camping trip was coming to an end, I still didn't want it to. But I was also appreciative of the memories we had created and the closer relationship we had developed. I felt a sensation of satisfaction come over me as we were driving back to our house and I peered out at the passing landscape. I knew that no matter what obstacles lay ahead, I would always have my family by my side, ready to face them with me.

It was time to get back to reality the next day. I experienced a wave of restlessness when my mother dropped me off at school on her way to work. Following the exhilaration of the camping trip, the prospect of returning to my normal routine left me with a sense of dread. Feeling out of place, I wandered through the corridors of my school. I felt suffocated by walls and fluorescent lights because I had been so engrossed in nature for the previous several days.

My thoughts kept returning to the events of the previous weekend as I sat in class and tried to concentrate on the things being taught. I reflected on the times we had spent together as a family and the joy and love that had filled our hearts. Yet now that I was a student, I had to deal with the realities of homework, tests, and all the other menial activities that went along with it. I could not stomach the prospect of spending my days immersed in workbooks and textbooks.

I was sitting at my desk, looking aimlessly through my textbooks, and I couldn't help but long for the freedom and excitement of the previous weekend. Yet I was aware that it was only a momentary sensation and that if I wanted to be successful in the future, I needed to concentrate on the here and now.

With a sigh, I opened my textbook and began to study, determined to do my best even if it wasn't as exciting as camping in the countryside. I knew that there would be more adventures to come, but for now, I had to focus on the task which is in my hand.

My best friend, Darshani, approached my desk while I was sitting in class, bored and restless. She gave me a cheeky grin, and I couldn't help but return the gesture.

She called out, "Heyyy Daisy, what's up?" with a hint of eagerness in her voice.

I said, rolling my eyes, "Not much, just trying to survive the dullness of school."

Laughing, Darshani. "I know, correct?" "I can hardly wait till the weekend."

The next several minutes were spent talking and sharing tales about our weekends. We spoke at the same pitch as always, and it was comforting to have someone who so completely understood me. Lucy, another buddy, came over to join us just as we were getting into our talk. Lucy was a friend from the neighbourhood, and while we weren't as close as Darshani and I, we still liked each other's company.

"What's up, fellas?" Lucy asked, plopping down at the desk next to me.

"Not much, just trying to get through class," I responded, smiling at her.

Lucy agreed with a shrug. "Yes, I agree. This math is destroying me."

We spent the next few minutes lamenting our mutual dislike of arithmetic, and then the bell sounded, signalling the end of class. I was glad for my friends' support and camaraderie as we grabbed our belongings and exited the classroom. Even if the school was tedious, having them at my side made it less so.

I couldn't help but feel pleased as we strolled down the corridor, conversing and joking. Whatever obstacles lay ahead, I knew I had my friends on my side, ready to face them alongside me. I couldn't help but roll my eyes as I stepped into my arithmetic class and saw our instructor, Mr Johnson, already standing at the front of the room, ready to begin the lesson.

I took my seat and got out my notepad, preparing to sit through another monotonous hour of mathematics. When Mr Johnson began his lesson, my mind wandered, thinking about other things. I couldn't help but marvel at why every math instructor was always on schedule!

Perhaps math teachers are born with an internal time clock that made them hyper-aware of the passing minutes and seconds. Or perhaps they were simply naturally obsessed with timetables and routines. I couldn't help but feel frustrated as I attempted to return to the lecture. Math was never my favourite subject, and I found it difficult to grasp the ideas and formulas.

But then, as Mr Johnson began to describe a particularly difficult subject, something snapped in my head. I suddenly realized what he was talking about, and I felt a burst of joy and pride. Maybe math wasn't that horrible after all. Maybe all it required was a little patience and effort, as well as the appropriate teacher to assist me through it. As I walked out of math class that day, I felt a surge of confidence. Maybe I couldn't answer every difficulty flawlessly, but all that mattered was that I was capable of learning and evolving.

Now It was my literature lesson, and I was filled with excitement and expectation. This was no ordinary lesson; it was the one subject that inspired my interest and imagination.

Our class was truly impressive, not just because of the subject content, but also because of our teacher, Ms Parker. If my life narrative had been written by a porangi author, Ms Parker would have been one of my most beloved characters.

Ms Parker was a literary virtuoso, with a passionate love of the written word that inspired and motivated me. Ms Parker made every session fascinating and thought-provoking, whether we were delving into Shakespeare's sonnets or examining the symbolism in "To Kill a Mockingbird". Yet it wasn't simply her intelligence and competence that distinguished Ms Parker. It was also her warmth and friendliness, as well as her ability to connect on a personal level with each of her kids.

Ms Parker was always ready to listen and provide advice if I had a problem or felt lost or confused. She had faith in me and my talents, and her unfailing support gave me the courage to follow my ambitions.

I felt a feeling of purpose and belonging as I sat in her class, surrounded by the smell of ancient books and the gentle rustle of turning pages. In a world of words and ideas, led by a teacher who saw the potential in each of us, this was where I belonged.

I grabbed my belongings as my literature lesson drew to a conclusion and walked out into the corridor as the last bell sounded. My two closest friends, Darshani and Lucy, were there to receive me.

As we made our way to the door, we strolled side by side along the well-known hallways while joking about our crushes. We were happy to be out of the rigidity and regularity of school, but on the other, we knew we would miss each other till the next day. This was how it always felt when we left for the day.

We took a big breath of fresh air as we walked outside into the direct sunlight before beginning to go along the street. What we were going to do for the rest of the day came up in our talk.

Darshani exclaimed joyfully, "I heard there's a new ice cream parlour that just opened up.

Lucy smiled and said, "I'm up for anything."

As we moved through the streets, we passed recognizable homes and stores. It was a lovely day, and the sun's warmth felt wonderful on our skin. While we strolled and spoke, I felt glad for the simple joy of spending time with friends. Being around individuals who were familiar with you well, who recognized your quirks and shared your emotions, was soothing!

We eventually made it to our houses, said our goodbyes, and agreed to make frameworks of madness for the next day. I had a wave of contentment as I shut the door behind me. Even if life wasn't always simple, moments like this were worth it.

I saw that a month had already gone since my dad returned from his vacation when I turned to look at the calendar that was hanging on the wall. As an army veteran, I understood that his time with us would be short. I wanted to enjoy it to the fullest. My father is my hero; he bravely and honourably served our nation, and I have always been in awe of him. Every time he returned home, I had a difficult-to-express sensation of pride and delight.

Yet at the same time, I realized that his time with us was brief. He would soon have to return to his duties, and we would be left behind to wait for his next visit. I couldn't help but feel melancholy as I considered his impending departure. But I also realized that I had to make the most of the time we had left.

The remainder of the day was spent doing things my dad and I enjoyed, including playing board games, watching movies, and simply conversing about life. That was straightforward, yet sufficient. As the days passed, I cherished every second I spent with him. We took lengthy strolls, travelled to new locations, and spoke about our own experiences. I was aware that I would always remember these moments.

It was then time for him to leave, which came all too quickly. We exchanged parting hugs as I felt tears well up in my eyes. I wanted him to stay, not to go. But he assured me that he would return soon, so I knew I had to have patience. Although the wait would be challenging, it would be worthwhile to see him once more. I had a range of feelings as I saw him go, including grief, desire, as well as pride and appreciation. My father was my idol, and I was aware of the significant contribution he was making to our nation. I would be proud as I waited for him.

The next day, I visited my buddy Lucy at her home. I was curious to see what Lucy had been working on because she has always been interested in gardening. Her front entrance was surrounded by a lovely assortment of flowers, which I saw as I approached it. I was eager to see what else Lucy had in mind because it was obvious that she had been working hard.

When Lucy answered the door, she seemed excited, and I could see it. She walked me outside to her backyard, where I was met with an amazing sight. A rainbow of colours was exploding from every nook and cranny of the whole garden, which was in full flower. Rows of flowers, trees, and even a tiny pond with fish swimming in it could be seen there. I was astounded by Lucy's skill at gardening. She liked spending time in her garden and had a genuine green thumb. Lucy sheepishly told me as we strolled around the yard that she was planting flowers for her future lover. I playfully poked her, wondering who this strange man was, but she blushed and refused to tell me.

Lucy's father came out to welcome us at that point. He, too, served in the army, and I could see the pride in his eyes as he talked about it. While we talked with Lucy's father, I couldn't help but feel grateful for the sacrifices he and my father made to serve our nation. It was an honour to know both of them.

When the day came to an end, I said my goodbyes to Lucy and her father, vowing to return soon. I couldn't help but feel at ease and satisfied as I headed home. Life is full of obstacles, but times like this make it all worthwhile.

Love you,

Daisy

:)

Chapter 2. Your Diary

Dear Anne,

On a study visit to a nearby bookshop the following day, when my class was there. I had the wonderful opportunity to delve into the realm of literature since the bookstore was brimming with books by writers and genres of all kinds. I was awestruck by the sheer quantity of books available as we browsed the aisles. Yet, "The Diary of a Young Girl" by Anne Frank attracted my attention as one book in particular.

Though I was familiar with your name "Anne Frank" I had never read about your diary. Our English instructor, Ms Parker, observed my interest in the book and recommended that I should purchase it. I took the book in my hand and began leafing through the pages. I could sense the agony and adversity that you had gone through throughout the war because of the writing's honesty and rawness. I was grateful to Ms Parker for proposing this book since I felt it would be necessary for me to read.

I noticed numerous writers and publishers marketing their books as we moved on through the bookstore. Learning about the publication process and the effort that went into writing a book was lengthy and fascinating. Yet I couldn't help but think about your diary. I was compelled to read it to find out more about your story.

I clutched your book carefully as the study trip drew to a conclusion and we made our way back to school, eager to begin reading and continue my literary exploration. I was immediately impressed by how gorgeous your diary's cover was as I noticed the large title "The Diary of a Young Girl" on it. I was intrigued by your cover picture since it perfectly reflected your childhood and purity.

I was astounded to see a girl of my age had created such a potent and touching narrative as I paged through your book. That was all the more astounding since you wrote it during such a terrible and hazardous period. I tried to understand what it must have been like for young Anne to spend two years in hiding with her family and friends, unable to leave or lead a typical life. And yet, despite all that difficulty and anxiety, you still had the fortitude to express your ideas and feelings in writing.

I was lured more and more into "Creative Anne's realm" as I began to read it. You wrote in a genuine, sincere manner that allowed me to get a sense of what life was like during the conflict. I was aware that reading "The Diary of a Young Girl" would be difficult and emotionally taxing, but I was also eager to find out more about you and your experience. The book's cover had initially caught my eye, and now the words within were winning my heart.

I couldn't stop feeling a strong connection to you as I kept reading your diary. Few other books have ever connected with me the way your feelings and experiences have. I had experienced the heartache of loss and the perplexity of growing up in a world that didn't always make sense, just like you had. I could relate to your young age, your frustration with your family, your troubles in school, and your yearning for more out of life.

Reading your diary was like laughing with a best friend who could relate to me in a way that no one else could. Your sentiments touched the very core of my spirit because they were sincere and honest. I started to compose letters to you in my brain, and I also want to share my daily musings with someone, much like you did with your diary (Kitty). I thus decided to write to you because I wanted to share my personal experiences with you and ask you some questions about yourself.

When I continued reading, I realized that your tale would stick with me for a long time. Your bravery and tenacity in the face of terrible suffering inspired me, and I was thankful to have had the opportunity to read your words and learn from your example. I had finished "The Diary of a Young Girl" after a week of reading and was ready to tell someone about it. I chose to discuss my feelings with my literature instructor, Ms Parker.

Ms Parker smiled and nodded when I told her how profoundly the book had affected me. "I'm delighted to hear that, Daisy," she said. "Anne Frank's diary is a moving witness to the human psyche." We chatted about Anne's narrative and the ideas that struck a chord with me for a time. Ms Parker provided her views and ideas, and I listened closely, happy for the opportunity to learn from her.

Ms Parker offered me a little grin as our talk came to an end. "I think you have a literary skill, Daisy," she replied. "Maybe you'll be the one penning novels that inspire people one day."

I felt a flush of pleasure as I walked away from our chat, and I realized she could be correct. If Anne Frank's diary taught me anything, it was that words have the power to transform and inspire. And who knows what type of influence I could have on the world if I could harness that power myself?

I began writing to you the next day as a method to convey my own emotions and seek companionship via the words of someone who had experienced similar emotions. I poured my heart out on the pages of my notebook, giving my hopes and worries, dreams and disappointments, and anything else that may be related to us.

The same day, I walked to Lucy's house to ask her for some flower seeds for my garden. Lucy was always willing to share her enthusiasm for gardening with me, and I learned a lot from her. I couldn't help but tell her about the letters I'd been writing to you while we chatted.

Lucy was captivated by the concept and requested to read some of the letters. I was scared about sharing my work with others, but I was also ecstatic at the thought of someone else reading my writings. I agreed to bring some of the letters over to her place the next time I visited.

As I went home, I reflected on how significant the letters had become in my life. Writing to you gave me a place to vent my feelings and views about the world, and it seemed like a personal connection to someone who had been through so much. I was glad for the opportunity to share my writing with Lucy, and I was inspired to keep writing letters to you.

As the days went by, my school examinations approached, and my anxiety grew. My mother continually reminded me of my low academic achievement and chastised me for not paying enough attention to my studies. Yet I couldn't help but be bored with the traditional academic program. I aspired to be a writer like 'The Anne Frank', writing works that would inspire and engage readers with tales of imagination and adventure.

I would find peace in sending letters to you every day. I'm not sure who will publish my top-secret letters in the future as your father did. I'm genuinely pouring my heart and soul out to you about my hopes and goals. I can tell you about my passion for writing and how I hoped to make it a career. In my letters, I would seek your advice and erudition, hoping that you might share some of your knowledge with me!

Now that exams were over my head, my anxiety grew even more. I knew I wasn't prepared enough, but I couldn't find the urge to study. I only wanted to write and read books like you did during your time in hiding. Yet I knew I had to do well in my examinations, not just for the sake of my mother and father but also for my future.

I attempted to concentrate on my academics, but my mind kept wandering to ideas of writing and my ambitions to become a writer. I was curious if you had ever felt the same way, whether you had battled to balance your aspirations and duties.

On the day of my result, I was apprehensive and nervous. I knew my grades were going to be bad, and I was worried about what my family and relatives would think. As soon as the results were announced, my phone began to ring nonstop with calls from family members inquiring about my grades. They seemed to be just concerned with the figures and not with how I was feeling or what I planned to do in the future!

Despite my lack of desire, I studied enough to pass my examinations, but not with flying colours. Yet I knew that my love of writing would always sustain me, and I would continue to write letters to you in whatever circumstance, seeking your advice and inspiration.

I was depressed and disappointed with myself, and my mother was upset with me for not studying hard enough. Yet deep inside, I felt that writing was my genuine love, not academia. Like you, I wanted to write stories that would inspire others. I desired to construct a universe in which everything was possible.

Despite my low grades, I opted to pursue my love of writing. I began spending more time composing stories and poetry, and I even began sending letters to my country's education minister! Indeed, I have determined not to give up on my aspirations.

After much scolding from my mom and even from the teacher, I planned to balance my schoolwork with my hobbies. I will be a nice daughter to my parents. Since then, I've reduced my leisure activities and monitored my timetable. The outcomes of such routines changed dramatically. I went from being a moronic kid who got single digits on tests to being third in my class. One of my short stories was also published in a well-known national publication!

I began to fantasize about the day when my writings would be published in a weekly magazine and read by people from all over the world. I imagined the day when my stories would be taught in schools, motivating young minds to write and dream big. Even though I knew the road ahead would be long and difficult, I was determined not to give up on my aspirations.

After a month I was welcomed by the lovely scent of the newly blooming flowers as I entered my yard. When I planted the seeds that my friend Lucy had given me just a few months' prior, a smile spread over my face. Thanks to the love and attention, I showed them, those little seeds had grown into lovely blooms.

I experienced a wave of serenity. The vibrant flowers' petals glowed in the sunlight as they softly swung in the air. The jasmine was a bright white, and the roses were a rich shade of red. The lilies were a delicate shade of pink, while the marigolds offered a pop of orange.

Despite the individual beauty of each bloom, they all came together to form a stunning spectacle. I took a seat among the flowers, closed my eyes, and inhaled deeply. My lungs were filled with the fragrance of the flowers, and I got the impression that I had been taken to a tranquil place.

I then understood the full splendour of nature. The colour, the aromas, and the background singing of the birds all blended to offer me a sense of tranquillity that I had never felt before. And I felt that this was where I belonged as I sat there, surrounded by the delights of nature. I took my time examining each flower's complex patterns and vibrant petals. That again served as a zesty reminder to me that even the little things in life have the power to make us extremely happy and joyful.

I picked a few flowers to place in a vase inside my room since their vivid colours made the area feel alive. As I sat down in my garden to write my daily thoughts to fill the words in my letter to you, I couldn't help but feel thankful for having a decent page and my pen with which to write you. I hope my words can help you experience the beauty of my garden.

I felt a friendly shove from behind while I was absorbed in the beauty of the surroundings. Lucy was making fun of me for holding flowers in my hand. "Are these flowers for your future sweetheart, Daisy?" she inquired with a mischievous grin. She teased me, and I couldn't help but chuckle. "No, Lucy," I answered, "I just adore the tranquility and beauty of these flowers. They help me feel content and joyful." Lucy nodded and grinned; she recognized my appreciation of the modest pleasures in life.

As we made our way towards Lucy's house, I could feel the grief in her eyes as we continued strolling down the route while taking in the beautiful weather and soft breeze. It was never easy for Lucy and her family when her father was preparing to go to his army camp. Every time he had to leave on duty, I could only imagine how difficult it must be for them to say goodbye.

Although Lucy's mother gave us a kind smile as soon as we got to her house and welcomed us, it was clear that she was depressed. The atmosphere was stoic as we sat down and spoke for a bit in the living room. In his uniform, Lucy's father entered the room. Following a bear embrace, he sat down next to his wife. He spoke about his impending mission and his hopes for changing things. Lucy sat next to him and gripped his hand firmly.

We all stood up to say farewell as he was about to depart. He was given a big cuddle by Lucy while she talked softly in his ear. Before departing, he smiled at her and hugged Lucy's mother. I could sense the weight in the air as we left the house. Although I was aware of how much Lucy and her family would miss him, I also had faith in their ability to overcome their loss as a unit.

Lucy and I both felt lighter as the fun week got closer. My joy knew no boundaries because the school festival was on my road. Everyone was excited to compete in the singing, dancing, and acting events at the next school festival.

When our class was given the task of decorating the entire school, we were all eager to show off our artistic talents.

We worked on our decorations for hours, cutting out bright papers and hanging them in the classrooms and hallways. As we collaborated to create a lovely and dynamic setting, the air was vibrating with enthusiasm and laughter.

When the day of the school festival approached, I experienced mixed emotions. I was going to participate in the school play, which was something new for me. I was sure I would succeed since I had practised my lines a hundred times!

We were all wearing our finest clothes on the day of the festival and prepared to display our skills. Everyone gave their performances throughout the intense singing and dance events.

The moment has finally arrived for us to perform. The audience was waiting while the stage was being prepared. I could feel my heart thumping rapidly while I was hiding behind the curtains. As soon as the curtains were drawn, I entered the stage. The audience was hushed, and the lights were brilliant. I inhaled deeply and started reciting my lines.

I became more and more certain as the drama went on. The crowd appeared to be enjoying it, and my fellow performers were doing an excellent job. The audience exploded in cheers as we finally reached the finale.

As we took our bow for the show, I had an adrenaline surge. I'll never forget the amazing feeling I experienced. I decided then and there that I wanted to keep performing, join the theatre club, and pursue my passion for the arts.

The higher-class pupils intended to bamboozle our math

teacher during the festival. Before he arrived at the podium to deliver his address, they put a whoopee cushion on his chair. As soon as he sat down, everyone started laughing because he farted loudly. Even the math teacher was unable to contain his laughter. We all laughed out loud since it was such a hilarious moment.

Yet the nicest part of the festival was watching the entire school come together, enjoying one other's company and having a good time. It was a clear indication of the value of unity and also how pulling together could result in something genuinely unique.

Summer break had finally arrived, and I couldn't wait to spend it all on writing and books. I went to the bookshop and purchased twenty novels of various genres, such as romance, mystery, fantasy, and thriller. My room was crammed with books, papers, and diaries. I spent my days immersed in the novels, taking notes and learning from the literary masters.

Every day, I spent hours writing, pouring my ideas into paper and expressing my creativity via words. My diary was constantly with me, and I wrote about anything that came to me, even the smallest facts. My fingers were continually scribbling, and I scribbled so much that the pages were nearly full.

I thought I was improving as a writer as the days went by. I was picking up new skills, enhancing my grammar, and increasing my vocabulary. Even though I had been daydreaming about writing my novel for a very long time, I finally got started.

I had the busiest summer break of my life, and I was proud of everything I had done. I was thankful for the chance to spend my time doing what I enjoyed, and I was certain that

I would keep writing for the rest of my life.

My head was buzzing with inventiveness as I began composing my novella. I used to lose hours of my life daydreaming about the exploits of my fictional characters. The protagonist of the tale was a young child named Poppy who lived in a tiny community in the forest. She came upon a massive, injured grizzly bear one day while playing in the wild. She assisted him, and they grew close.

The plot was influenced by the well-known animated series Masha and the Bear, which I enjoyed watching as a young child. I wanted to write a novel that would both amuse young readers and teach them valuable lessons about friendship and generosity.

My desk started to fill up with papers, notes, and pencils as I wrote. But I didn't care since I was absorbed in my little universe. The only time I would take a break was to read one of the books I had bought, which included timeless works like The Great Gatsby, Pride and Prejudice, and other works by Jane Austin. I felt encouraged, and my writing talents improved after reading these books.

I finished my novella at the end of my summer break, and I was pleased with the results. That was a gratifying experience that showed me the value of imagination and creativity. I went to my neighbourhood bookshop to inquire about the publishing process. The manager of the bookstore was a pleasant, elderly man who carefully listened to my question. He described to me how drawn-out and difficult the publication process is. He advised me to begin by locating a literary agent who could guide me through the procedure.

He provided me with a list of trustworthy literary agencies as well as advice on how to contact them. To hone my skill, he also advised that I go to various writing seminars. I expressed my gratitude for his counsel and walked out of the store feeling both thrilled and overjoyed. Although the idea of being a published author was exciting, the procedure appeared difficult.

Yet I was adamant that I would pursue my ambition and make it come true. I was in awe of it! I was going to get my short fantasy story published! I was feeling both anxious and excited at the same time. It took me a lot of time to write and edit, but finally, it was there for everyone to read. I was both proud of who I was and afraid of what other people could think.

The publisher was friendly and helpful. They took care of all the legal details and explained everything to my mom. I couldn't wait to see the finished product! I was interested in the cover and the artwork's final appearance.

Months seemed like days until the day finally came. My mother received a call from the publisher informing her that the books were prepared. We hurried to the bookstore, where my novella was waiting for us on a shelf. The picture of a little child cuddling a large, fluffy bear on the cover was lovely.

I had the impression that I was dreaming. I couldn't believe I was holding my book! I turned the pages and admired the pictures and the words I had written. I had the feeling of a true author. I'll forever remember that particular moment. I had a realization at that time that if I gained more experience and believed in myself, I could reach my objectives.

I was overjoyed and immensely proud of myself when my novella was published. I wished for everyone to read it and appreciate it. I decided to give every copy of my book to the orphanage and library in my city. I thought that everyone should be able to read and have access to literature, especially young people who would not otherwise have that opportunity. They should enjoy my book, and I hope it encourages them to read and write their own stories.

Even though my father was distant from his army duties, I couldn't wait to bring him my book. He needed to read my narrative to understand how much I cherished him. I painstakingly packed my book and wrote him a loving note, expressing my love and gratitude for having him as my father and how much I missed him. I thought that reading my book would make him smile while he was away from home.

When I discovered that my book was displayed on the same shelf as your book at the bookshop, I couldn't believe it. For me, it was like a dream come true. And to think that we both loved telling stories—you and I, both writers. I felt compelled to gift you a copy of my book that was specially autographed and dedicated to you. The least I could do as a friend and fellow writer.

Anne, I wanted to thank you for everything. My life has altered ever since I started sending letters to you. My newfound love for writing has given me a new direction in life. And now that my book has been released, I feel even closer to you. In the same way that your diary has inspired me, I hope that my book and our correspondence will continue to inspire others.

Love you,

Daisy

:)

Chapter 3. Take up Arms

Dear Anne,

I was ecstatic to see my father once he had finished his duty. After giving him a firm kiss, I led him to my garden. I showed him the stunning blooms that Lucy's seeds produced. Father was astounded by the appearance of my garden and thanked me for my dedication.

My father was informed about my book and the publishing process. He assured me that he would read it right away and expressed his great pride in me. He told me about the book that I had sent him, but due to an urgent mission, he was not able to read it. I also spoke to him about you and how my desire to write was sparked by your diary. Papa calmly listened to me and urged me to continue writing. We spoke about life, family, and dreams while spending the evening outside in the garden. I will always treasure that special moment in my heart since it was so lovely.

After a long summer break, it was a nice day, and I was looking forward to seeing my friends. As soon as I walked through the school gate, I saw Lucy and Darshani standing close to the entrance. We all gave each other hugs as I ran over to them. We got to chat about the books we read, the wonderful activities we did, and our summer vacation.

"I spent my summer vacation at my grandparent's home in the countryside in the hilly region," Darshani explained. We went on nature hikes, interacted with domesticated animals, and generally had a fine experience.

Lucy went on to say, "My family and I travelled to a beach resort. We went on a boat excursion, played in the water, and created sandcastles. It was a lot of fun!"

I smiled and said, "I spent most of my summer vacation writing my novella and reading books. I also helped my mother in the kitchen garden."

We spoke for a little longer before heading to our respective classrooms. It was fantastic to be back at school and see my classmates. After a long summer break, I was eager to see my pals. Darshani and Lucy were already seated at their desks when I entered the classroom. We exchanged delighted smiles and began our normal banter. We discussed our summer vacation and how we spent it once again. Darshani talked about her experience studying various dance forms.

Our teacher requested everyone share their vacation memories as the class began. Each student stepped up and spoke about their vacation experiences one by one. As David's turn came, he stepped up and made a witty comment that everyone laughed at. That was so hilarious that even the teacher couldn't help but laugh. We all laughed a lot and went back to our lectures.

My father decided that after we completed our supper, we would go out and have some ice cream. I was overjoyed about the idea, so I put on my shoes and we set off. The night was chilly and windy, with stars twinkling in the sky. We went for a walk to our favourite ice cream shop, which was only a few blocks away from our house. We struggled to choose between the numerous delectable flavours, but we eventually agreed on our favourites. We ate our ice cream, spoke about our day, and planned plans for the weekend as we strolled back home. That was a fantastic night, and I was glad to have such a lovely family.

As my father and I sat down to watch the news, I felt a knot in my stomach as the headlines screamed that our country was at war. It was unexpected for all of us, and we watched as news outlets reported on the escalation of hostilities between our country and another. Our country's authorities had proclaimed a state of emergency, and tensions were high. It was a terrifying period, and we were all filled with dread about what the future held.

When word of the conflict spread, the mood in our country grew tense and fearful. People were worried about their own and their loved ones' safety. Several households began stockpiling goods and preparing for the worst.

My father was summoned back to service amid all this mayhem. He had previously served in the war and was now being called upon to do so again. We were all shocked to get the news, but we understood it was his responsibility to serve his nation.

The news of the conflict got increasingly intense as the days passed. To keep civilians safe, the government imposed curfews and other security measures. Schools and universities were closed, forcing many individuals to stay indoors.

The majority of my time was spent reading books to escape the continual anxiety and terror that had overtaken our nation. It was hard for me to maintain optimism and hope when there were new reports of fatalities and damage every day.

The following day, from the top of the hill where my house was situated, I peered out the window and saw thick smoke rising in the distance. The fragrance reminded me of battle, and it pounded my heart. Look at all that smoke, Dolly, I said as I turned to face my doll. Sometimes, this world can be so harsh. Why is it so hard for people to just be kind to one another? I tightly grabbed my doll as I simultaneously felt scared and depressed. I found it hard to understand why people wanted to harm people and destroy property. All I want is for us to get along and be friends.

I wanted there to be no suffering brought on by conflict or bloodshed. Yet I was aware that my hopes wouldn't be enough to bring about the desired outcome. I sat there for a long time, contemplating all the wrongs in the world while I observed the smoke ascend. Even though I was just a young girl who is now playing with a doll, I was aware that I had to take action to change things, even if it was in a very modest way. I heard my parents conversing quietly as I was reading my books in my room. Outside, I could hear gunfire and explosions, but I was accustomed to this at this point. In the room next door, my father was arranging his belongings, while my mother was cooking dinner in the kitchen.

I listened to my parents talking while I played. My father's voice indicated that something significant was taking place, and it was serious. He came out of his room wearing his military garb, and I observed him. He took my hand and bent down in front of me. He said, "Daisy, my sweetheart, I must leave for a bit to defend our nation." So don't worry; everything will be good, and remember, everything is fair in war and love.

I raised an anxious, wide-eyed gaze at him.

"Daddy, is it necessary to go there and why?" I asked.

My father said, "Because occasionally there are wicked individuals who wish to harm our country. So don't fear; our family and you will always be safe since your father is a strong soldier."

"But, Daddy, someone's father must also be one of your adversaries. Would you murder him? He gave me a forehead kiss while grinning, then rose while carrying his suitcase. He told my mother, "I've got to go now. "Look after Daisy for me."

My mother nodded, her eyes filled with sorrow, and they hugged warmly as they said their goodbyes. I watched them as a wave of terror and grief swept over me. I questioned why individuals must fight and injure one another, as well as why my father must abandon us to battle. My mother and I closed our eyes and held hands as we sat in our living room. We prayed that my father would return from the war unscathed. My mother's palm felt clammy and chilly in mine, and I could feel my heart beating with fear. I saw in a newspaper that "top leaders and their families will be under heavy security during the conflict," which was one of the catchy headlines. I felt sad after seeing this.

We prayed to God to keep my father safe and return him to us. We prayed for endurance during this trying period, as well as for faith that everything would be okay. I couldn't help but think about the risks that my father would be taking while serving in the military. I questioned his well-being, his level of fear, and whether or not he missed us as much as we missed him. For some time, my mother and I sat in silence, both of us preoccupied with our worries. Yet we clung to one another, seeking solace in our common faith and hope.

I had a sense of tranquility as soon as our prayers ended. We realized that by turning to God and requesting his assistance, we had done everything we could to prevent the war's conclusion. When we gripped one another fiercely, I realized that as long as we had each other and our faith, everything would be well. We would never lose sight of the strength of love and hope in the face of hardship as we continued to pray and hope for my father's safe return.

My mother and I had a new challenge as the war continued: the increased cost of food. Everything appeared to be getting costlier every day, and the nation's financial woes caused my father's salary to be delayed. My mother and I had to start limiting our meals as a result. We would eat at the table while observing the small pieces that were placed in front of us. Though our bellies would grumble with hunger, we were aware that we needed to stretch out this food as much as we could. My mother was trying to figure out how to stretch our meagre means, and I could see the stress written over her face.

Using the little items, we had, we would make our tiny meals as nutrient-dense as we could. On occasion, we would feel the hunger pangs as we went to sleep with empty stomachs. We were going through a tough period, and it was terrible to see my mother struggle to make ends meet. My mother, however, persevered and stayed strong throughout. She would comfort me by telling me that everything would be OK and that all we had to do was keep moving forward in the direction of a brighter tomorrow.

We never forgot the value of love, family, and community in difficult times, even though our meals were meagre and we had few resources. We would strive to help one another through difficult times by sharing what little we had with our neighbours. In the end, it was our fortitude and capacity for unity that saw us through the difficult times of war and famine. We were confident that we would prevail and that we would never forget the lessons we had learned about the strength of love and tenacity.

I was stunned to hear that Lucy's father had died in the war. I knew that something dreadful had happened when I heard the shrill wail coming from my neighbour's home. My friend's father passed away, and I was devastated for her and her family. The atmosphere during the burial, though, was even more devastating. These lovely flowers, which my Lucy had planted for her future lover, were now being placed on her father's body as he was being laid to rest. Long after the funeral was finished, I was left with a poignant and horrifying memory.

I was overcome by emotion as I made my way back to my home. The idea of my flowers being utilized in such a manner was intolerable to me. In the face of such loss and pain, they at once looked inconsequential and trivial. So I pulled all of my flowers out of the ground with my gardening equipment. Even though it was simply a tiny act, I thought it was the only way I could honour my friend and her family and express my support for them. I had a new perspective on the world that day. I came to understand how fleeting life may be and how crucial it is to treasure the time spent with our loved ones. In moments of tragedy and loss, I have also seen the impact of modest gestures and deeds of compassion. I was always reminded to cherish the beauty in life and to never take anything for granted by the memories of my friend's father and the flowers she had raised.

After a month I got a letter from my father. As I opened the letter from my father, my heart sprang with happiness and relief. I was initially excited, but as soon as I opened the package and saw the blood spots on the paper, my pleasure was quickly replaced with horror. I read my father's words as he attempted to reassure me that everything was fine, but I knew he was lying. His remarks had a palpable feeling of fear and sorrow, and I realized that he had to be experiencing an indescribable amount of suffering.

I couldn't help but ponder my father's situation and the level of danger he was in throughout the war. My concern and anxiety were further heightened by the blood splatters on the letter. I stumbled outside while crying and passed out next to the garden. Without any idea of what to do or how to assist my father, I felt utterly useless and alone. Even yet, I was aware that I needed to maintain my composure for the sake of my family. I brushed away my tears and exhaled deeply as I searched for some sort of inner calm and resolution.

I was aware that my father was depending on me to uphold his moral principles and keep our family together while he was gone. I took a deep breath and told myself to keep going and never give up. The garden's beauty and tenacity also reminded me that there is always hope for fresh growth and rejuvenation, even in the most difficult circumstances. With the relatively small amount of money my father had sent in the letter, it was obvious that we would need to find a means to get by until he got back from the war.

After talking about our choices with my mother, we decided that the only way to support our family was to sell everything we owned. We began by attempting to sell some of our stuff, such as jewellery and clothing, but quickly found that we also needed to sell furniture and other home items. We had a tough and painful process as we observed how our house gradually became bare and empty. Yet we understood that it was essential to get by until my father came home.

We made an effort to remind ourselves as we sold each item that these things were the only things in the world and that what counted most was our family's love and unity. Even if we didn't have much else, we knew that we would always have each other. We also learned the value of hard work and ingenuity as we banded together to make ends meet. We developed more inventive methods to stretch our resources and save money, including growing our veggies and repairing our clothing rather than buying new ones. Eventually, we were able to get through those trying times. Looking back, I see that those trying circumstances helped me learn valuable lessons about tenacity, fortitude, and the genuine value of family.

I was so anxious about the battle that I didn't see my mother's condition getting worse. One evening after supper, I overheard her coughing loudly in her room. As I went to check on her, I discovered that she was having trouble breathing. I contacted my neighbour right away, and they hurried her to the hospital.

We were informed by the hospital that my mother had a serious case of lung cancer. The physicians explained that she had not taken her medication since it was so expensive. I was absolutely distraught, and I felt I had to act to assist.

I got in touch with my relatives and asked them to collect the necessary funds to cover my mother's medical expenses. She spent a few weeks in the hospital, but the doctor continually gave me the runaround. That was a difficult period for me, and I realized that the war was not the only difficulty I was dealing with. We were advised to leave the hospital because we couldn't afford the hospital's pharmaceutical costs.

After a month I was crushed to hear that my mother's sickness was approaching its conclusion. I felt afraid and helpless since I didn't know how to help her. As my mother couldn't take care of herself due to her sickness, I had to take on additional responsibilities at home. Although I did my best to look after her, it was tough to see her in agony and realize that there wasn't anything I could do to stop it. I decided to sell some of my produce one day so I could buy my mother's medications. I believed that if I could only improve her, everything else would take care of itself.

Yet as the days passed, my mother's health kept getting worse. She grew frailer and frailer, and I could see the suffering in her eyes. I once slept next to her while firmly gripping her hand. Her hold on my hand was slipping away from her, but I clung to it. She ignored my calls for her, despite my calls for her. I discovered that my mom had died in her sleep the next morning. I was crushed and inconsolable, thinking that a piece of me had died along with her.

Even in my pain, I knew my mother would want me to be strong and continue ahead. I understood that her greatest gift to me had been the love and sacrifice she had shown me throughout her life and that I would always carry her memories with me. And as I glanced about, I was struck by nature's beauty and tenacity, which reminded me that even in the face of loss and tragedy, there is always hope for fresh growth and rejuvenation.

I felt lonely and sad as I sat alone in my house, holding a photo of my mother and missing my parents dreadfully. Without my mother's presence, the home felt empty, and I had no idea if my father was okay or when he would return from the war. With the sun setting outside and darkness falling, the evening felt especially lonely. I tried reading your diary to divert myself, but nothing held my interest.

I was instead absorbed in my thoughts, thinking back on the pleasant times I had spent with my parents before the war. I realized how much I had taken for granted the times we had shared while laughing and playing games. Yet now that they were gone, I saw how much I had relied on my parents for solace and support. I had no idea how to get around in the world by myself, and the war's uncertainty made matters worse.

I became aware that I needed to find a means to deal with my loneliness and dread as I sat there alone in the evening. I was aware that even though they weren't here, my parents would want me to be resilient and carry on. I decided to concentrate on the good times and teachings that my parents had imparted to me and to draw strength from those memories as I confronted the challenges that lay ahead. And while I clutched my mother's picture in my hand, I felt at ease knowing that she was keeping an eye on me, even from the other side.

Love you,

Daisy

:)

Chapter 4. My Quest

Dear Anne,

I was worried and anxious since I hadn't heard from my father in more than five months. I knew I had to find a method to find him because the idea of him being lost and in danger was too painful for me to take. I decided to search for my father, and thus I left early one morning. I gathered my doll for comfort, packed some food and other necessities, and started on my quest. The trek was laborious and drawn out, with numerous hazards and challenges to overcome. I had to manoeuvre through perilous areas and cross hazardous terrain while constantly on high alert for any signals of danger.

Yet I was determined to track out my father and return him to safety, whatever the challenges. I was prepared to go to all lengths necessary to assure his safe return, even though I knew it would be a challenging and dangerous trek. The memories we had created as a family came to me as I walked, and I realized how much I missed his warm hug and consoling words. I prayed for his protection and well-being in the hopes that my search would bring me to him and that we might be together once more.

I never lost hope, even as hours turned into days and days into weeks. I kept moving across the challenging and punishing terrain, looking out for my father's whereabouts at all times. The unending rows of vertical stones commemorating the graves of those who had perished in the battle made my heart sink as I went past the cemetery. It served as a sharp reminder of the terrible toll that the war had taken on our neighbourhood and the numerous lives it had claimed.

The agony and pain that must be experienced by all the families who have lost loved ones kept coming to mind. It served as a depressing reminder that the only people who seemed to benefit from the war were the undertakers and coffin makers, which made money off of all the graves. My attention then shifted to my own family and the anxiety and dread that had engulfed us ever since my father had enlisted in the military. The prospect of losing him was intolerable, and the sight of the cemetery just strengthened my resolve to track him down and return him to his family. When I passed through another cemetery, one stone stuck out from the rest. That was the same stone that my friends and I had used to play hide and seek without comprehending the marker's actual importance. Standing in front of it now, I felt a strong sense of grief and loss, because it was used as a memorial to those who perished in battle.

On the stone, the names of the soldiers were etched. I looked up my father's name. My fingers were shaking as I pointed to the stones. When my father's name was not mentioned, I felt a sensation of calm run down my spine. It was a sharp reminder that the repercussions of war were all too real and that innocent children's lives were not immune to their devastation. I went on my trek with renewed zeal, knowing that each step moved me closer to locating my father and returning him home to safety.

I moved cautiously along the street as the troops raced by in front of me. I noticed smoke billowing into the sky as I got closer to the bookshop. I became aware of what was going on, and my heart sank. The heat from the flames became nearly intolerable as I drew nearer. I could see books and papers burning in the streets, and the entire bookstore was engulfed in flames. People's screams and sobs could be heard above the thick, suffocating smoke.

On the opposite side of the street, I noticed some individuals huddling close together and watching in fear as the building burned to the ground. My heart broke for the mother I saw holding a young infant in her arms and weeping. I wanted to assist, but I had no idea how.

The distant sound of gunshots and explosions evoked recollections of the conflict that was ripping our nation apart. I felt a sense of sadness come over me as I realized it would be much harder to find my father than I had anticipated.

Yet I was aware that I couldn't give up. I had to keep going despite the challenges I encountered. Therefore, despite all odds, I proceeded on my trek while carrying a heavy heart in the hopes that I would eventually come across my father.

Oh oh, my school! It was obliterated. Rubble and trash filled the once-bustling hallways. Desks and chairs were strewn across the classrooms, which were no longer identifiable. At recess, we used to play on the playground, but now it was just a mess of broken swings and slides.

I was seeing things that I couldn't believe. As I considered all the memories I had created in that school, my heart plummeted. The moments I had shared with my friends, the knowledge I had gained, and the joy and sorrow of children's shouts and laughter echoed as I moved through the wreckage, giving the impression that the school was still in operation. But then I saw that it was all in my head. People were screaming and shouting all around me as they searched for their loved ones and attempted to rescue what they could from the rubble.

So much suffering and ruin had been caused by the conflict. All I could do at that point was hope and pray for my father's safety. When I saw the ice cream shop, hotels, and amusement park that I used to visit with my family utterly destroyed by the war, I couldn't believe my eyes. The streets, which had formerly been busy, were now empty and littered with trash. The ice cream shop was in ruins, and the rides at the amusement park were twisted and broken.

When I saw people roaming the area in search of their loved ones or any leftover goods, a knot in my throat developed. Despair and a feeling of loss pervaded the atmosphere. It served as a vivid reminder of how innocent civilians' daily lives are negatively impacted by conflict. I pondered how many lives were lost, how many homes were damaged, and how many families were impacted.

Geez, such a depressing scene! Everything has been destroyed by the conflict. My school was completely destroyed as I drove by it. The hotels, amusement parks, ice cream shops, bookstores, hospitals, schools, malls, and whatnot were all destroyed. It resembled a deserted town where there had previously been a thriving population.

I was so frantic to reach my friend Darshani's house and take refuge there, but to my shock, it was abandoned. The place was empty. It was devastating. I was sorely missing my pals, and I couldn't stop remembering our enjoyable days together. I prayed that they were safe someplace and hoped they were.

I was lost and alone. All of my friends and family were gone, my mother was gone, and my father was nowhere to be seen. I was clueless as to what to do or where to go. I was simply aimlessly walking the city, feeling hollow and numb. There was incessant gunfire and explosion noise in the distance, the streets were desolate, and the buildings were completely demolished.

The only thing I had on me was a picture of my mother, which I held close to my chest. In this chaotic and ruined world, it was the only thing that brought me any peace. I had a twinge of desire and melancholy as I gazed at her happy smile in the picture. I hoped she was here with me so she could lead me and shield me from the dangers all around me.

Yet I was aware that it was impossible. Even though it seemed like I was walking through a never-ending nightmare, I had to maintain my strength and continue. No matter how difficult it would be, I had to confront whatever the future had for me. I thus took a deep breath, wiped away my tears, and proceeded on my quest in the hope that I might one day see my father and discover new hope in this desolate world.

Seeing such disparities in our country was heartbreaking. The wealthy and strong were shielded, while the weak and defenceless were left on their own. It didn't seem right that those who struggled to make ends meet during difficult times suffered the most. People were begging for food and shelter on the streets as I passed by; their once-comfortable lives had been reduced to basic survival. I began to ponder why there couldn't be justice and equality for everyone, irrespective of socioeconomic standing.

I can recall a period when a modest sum of money could buy a variety of goods, but now, despite having plenty of cash, I am unable to purchase even a bottle of purified water. Even essentials have become prohibitively costly due to the country's severe inflationary crisis. In times of war and strife, the average person suffers the most. It's unfair that those who are in charge of all this carnage and turmoil are enjoying life in style while the rest of us are struggling to get by. I wish there was a way to return our lives to a state of calm and normalcy.

I had ragged clothing on that barely covered my flesh. My feet were often hurting from walking on uneven ground, and my shoes were full of holes. To shield myself from the smoke and dust, I had a scarf wrapped around my head. Due to my continual exposure to the harsh climate, my hands were rough and dry. My mother's picture, my dolly and a handful of my possessions, and some scavenged food were all I took with me in a little bag. While I was aware of how I seemed to be living on the streets, it was the best I could do at the time.

Yet despite the difficulties, I made an effort to uphold some form of standard. I would wash my face with what little water I had and put a ribbon in my hair that was still in good shape. In the middle of all the turmoil and damage all around me, it wasn't much, but it did help me feel a bit better about myself.

As I noticed my image in the mirror, I was startled. My once-healthy, chubby body has suddenly turned skeletal and weak. I was wearing baggy clothing and could feel my bones poking through my skin. I struggled to identify myself and was overcome by sadness at how drastically my look had changed. My physical damage from the conflict served as a stinging reminder of the terrible reality I was experiencing.

Anne, I wish you were here because I miss you. I wish the conflict would finish quickly so that everything could return to normal. I'll keep writing to you till then and am hoping to hear from you shortly.

Love you,

Daisy

:)

Chapter 5. Love & War

Dear Anne,

I was fatigued now, having been on the road for two weeks. My biscuit and snack packets were nearly empty. I sat down beneath the tree and fell asleep for a bit.

Indeed, I did find my father! My father and I sat down to catch up on everything that has transpired since he left. I informed him about the difficulties my mother and I had endured, such as rising food prices and her mother's illness and death. I broke the tragic news to him about our neighbour's father, who had perished in the war. Father listened closely, his heart heavy with grief for all the anguish and suffering his family has endured while he has been away. He tells me about his troubles and the atrocities he has encountered on the battlefield.

The sound of a bomb and shooting startled me awake. I was dreaming that I couldn't see my father anywhere, that I was in a danger zone, and that there was fire all around me. I was so perplexed that I ran towards the secure zone, where all citizens were stationed. One lovely lady handed me a piece of bread, and her grin reminded me of my mother. I wanted to thank her, but she had gone into the midst of the mob.

There was a lot of noise and turmoil around me. People were yelling and rushing about, and everything was dusty and black. If my mother was still alive, I could clutch her hand strongly. I wandered for days and nights until I reached the refugee camp. The camp was not at all like home. There were no pleasant sounds or vivid colours. The air was thick with melancholy and misery. I saw folks that looked exhausted and terrified, just like us, wherever I looked. The tents were crammed, and there was little room to manoeuvre.

I slept on the hard ground since the evenings were freezing. I didn't always have enough food to eat, and my stomach hurt all the time. I missed my pals and my books, but the most important thing was that I missed feeling protected. But even amid the darkness, I discovered hope. I met other youngsters who had lost their homes and families, just like me. We played games and sang songs together, and we forgot about the conflict outside for a time. We had each other, and that was all we needed. I'm not sure what will happen next, but I know I'll keep fighting for my life. My mother always said I'd find my father one day, and I believe her. Until then, I'll cherish our old memories and hope for a brighter future.

The officer of the refugee camp informed us one day about the battalion that was going to arrive today to give over the dead to loved ones. My father was also a member of the same battalion. I was so stressed out watching this, and as time went on, my heart began to fill up with more blood. At the moment, I was praying to God with every breath I took. I didn't feel hungry or thirsty. I want my father back because I adore him. It's been a year since I've seen him. After a day, the truck came, and two soldiers from the truck began to take down the dead.

As the corpse was brought down, the hearts of those who loved it were also taken down. I was alone in the crowd as the names of the deceased were read aloud. My father's name was missing after I took all the names. I breathed a sigh of relief. When one soldier reported to the officer, he was told, "Sir, we have one more body, but the name is not recorded on the list. The troops took down the body. I let out a scream after viewing this. My father lay still on the ground. Both of his hands were missing. He wasn't responding to me. I was not able to hold his hands.

I was screaming. I was crying, and I had no idea what to do. I grabbed my father so closely that I couldn't hear his heartbeat any more. Mom and dad, I cursed God more than Satan because you both left me in this horrible world and I could no longer hear both of your heartbeats.

His hands were gone: his hands, through which he could curl my entire body and make me feel safe; his hands, which were always kissed by my mother; his hands, which taught me to give others my hands for help; his hands, which could be my bodyguard; and his hands, which always made me smile when I was sad.

Dad No, you are the biggest liar in the world. "Nothing is fair in love or war."

Anne, I know you've made your diary a best-seller. You are now famous! Yet, like you, I had a tragic past. I'm writing to thank you for listening to my story about the things I've gone through. Anne, I could see the tears from your gorgeous eyes pouring onto the page as you read this.

I've learned as a 14-year-old girl that literature is a dimension within itself, existing exclusively between the pages of books. It is a fantasy world where anything is possible, where heroes can beat insurmountable challenges, and where the weak can defeat the strong. Unfortunately, that is not how the world that we live in is.

There are no fairy godmothers to grant wishes or magic spells to fix our troubles in our world. Instead, we deal with issues like poverty, prejudice, and violence in everyday life. These are issues that cannot be resolved by merely picking up a book or repeating a passage from it.

While literature may offer us direction and inspiration, it cannot be a panacea for all of our difficulties. Efforts must be made in order to improve the world. We must fight for justice, speak out against injustice, and work to create a society that is more fair and inclusive.

In a society that can be so unkind and merciless, it is easy to give up hope, but we must never forget that we can change things. We may utilize the knowledge and understanding we get from literature to direct our efforts as we try to make the world a better place. As a girl, I believe that it is up to us to take action and work towards creating a world that is more just, equitable, and compassionate.

I've learned that life can be unpredictable and occasionally unjust, especially when it comes to love and war. These two aspects of the human experience are frequently viewed as venues in which individuals must fight for what they desire, no matter the consequences.

When it comes to chasing the object of our passion, we frequently hear the saying "All's fair in love and war," which indicates that everything goes. This can lead to people acting deceptively, manipulatively, or even hurtfully toward others in the name of love or war. Yet, this type of behaviour is neither healthy nor sustainable, and it can have long-term consequences for both the individual and the relationship.

Similarly, in times of conflict, we frequently witness individuals going to extraordinary lengths to win the victory, regardless of the human cost. Acts of violence, devastation and even genocide are examples of this. Although the saying "all's fair in love and war" might be used to defend such behaviours, there are limitations to what is permissible in battle. International law, for example, restricts the use of brutal weapons and techniques.

Last, while the adage "all's fair in love and war" conveys that there are no rules or restrictions to what we may do to attain our objectives, it is critical to remember that our actions have repercussions.

Don't worry Anne, I'm now in safe hands; I was moved to an orphanage after that. Now that I am living a great life, I have friends and a teacher who are constantly there for me. When I'm depressed, I simply read your diary. I like the way you've structured it. Your presence in my heart will always make me joyful and fearless. Yet, unfortunately, nothing changed in this world after your death. I'll beg God to let me be a fictitious character in someone else's story in my next life so that I can have a happy ending.

Love you,

Daisy J

Can I Ask a Favor

If you enjoyed this Novella and found it useful or otherwise, then I'd appreciate it if you would post a short review on your social media accounts. I do read all the reviews personally so that I can continually write what people are wanting.

If you'd like to leave a review then please email me at aryanahire28@gmail.com. Thanks for your support!